# Hello, First Grade

by Joanne Ryder
Pictures by Betsy Lewin

**Troll Associates**

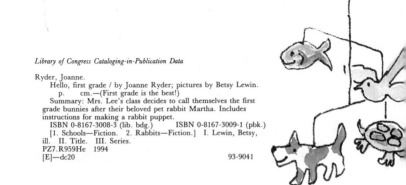

*Library of Congress Cataloging-in-Publication Data*

Ryder, Joanne.
 Hello, first grade / by Joanne Ryder; pictures by Betsy Lewin.
 p. cm.—(First grade is the best!)
 Summary: Mrs. Lee's class decides to call themselves the first
grade bunnies after their beloved pet rabbit Martha. Includes
instructions for making a rabbit puppet.
 ISBN 0-8167-3008-3 (lib. bdg.)   ISBN 0-8167-3009-1 (pbk.)
 [1. Schools—Fiction. 2. Rabbits—Fiction.] I. Lewin, Betsy,
ill. II. Title. III. Series.
PZ7.R959He 1994
[E]—dc20                                    93-9041

With thanks to the children, librarians and teachers of Jefferson and Lakeview Schools
in Norman, Oklahoma and Holy Family School in Rochester Hills, Michigan for their
spirited welcomes.

                                                                    JR

Text copyright © 1993 Joanne Ryder

Illustration copyright © 1993 Betsy Lewin

On the first day of school, the new first graders looked all around their classroom. It was a cheery place.

"I can read that sign," said Gabe. "It says, 'Hello, First Graders.'"

"Good morning," said their teacher.
"I am Mrs. Lee. Let's sit on the rug
and get to know each other."

"My front tooth fell out," said
Katie.

"Mine is very wiggly," said Meg.

"I'm new," said Nick. "We just moved here."

"I like cats," said Lisa.

"I have a twin," said Matt. "Mike looks just like me, but he can whistle."

After everyone finished, Mrs. Lee
said, "There is someone I want you to
meet."

"This is Martha," said their teacher.
"She is very gentle. If you are kind,
you can help take care of her."

Mrs. Lee often let Martha out of her cage. Soon the class was used to seeing the bunny hop by as they worked.

When Katie was reading on the rug, Martha licked her face.

"Your whiskers tickle," Katie told her, giggling.

Martha hopped over to Gabe and
sat on his puzzle. Everyone laughed.
"It's okay, Martha," said Gabe.
"My little sister does that, too."

One morning, Nick had a time out. He felt bad. But Martha came and tugged on his pants. She sat by him while he petted her. Soon he felt much better.

    As the weeks passed, the class
discovered things about Martha.
Often, she slept in her cage. But she
liked to take naps in other places, too.

"I found her," said Meg. "She was sleeping in my cubbyhole."

One day the principal visited them. "Friday is First Grade Day," she said. "Each class does something special. It's fun to see everybody's class spirit."

"We can make a special quilt for First Grade Day," Mrs. Lee told her class.

She gave them each a piece of cloth.

"Paint a picture of yourself or a friend in class," she said, "and I'll sew the pieces together."

Brian and Katie reached for the white paint. Everyone wanted white paint!

When Mrs. Lee saw the pictures, she smiled.

Martha was in each painting.

"Sometimes a class picks a special animal," said Mrs. Lee. "I think you just picked ours."

"We could be the first grade bunnies," Robin said.

"We'll need bunny ears," said Nick.
"I can make them," said Brian.
He helped draw the ears. Nick and
Gabe cut them out.

Lisa showed the class how to make
bunny puppets.

"Our puppets have lots of spirit,"
Robin said, waving hers

On Friday Mrs. Lee's class was excited. They put on their bunny ears and carried their puppets proudly.

Meg and Gabe carried a big basket. Their class quilt was inside.

"You all look wonderful," said
Mrs. Lee. "Now let's get Martha."
"Where is she?" asked Katie.
Martha was missing!

The children helped each other think of Martha's hiding places. They looked for her together, but could not find her.

Matt even went next door to Mike's class. But Martha wasn't there.

"We'll find her later," said Mrs. Lee. "I'm sure she's just taking a nap somewhere."

The first grade bunnies were quiet as each class took its turn on stage.

When it was their turn, the class lined up. No one smiled. It was hard to feel happy when Martha was missing.

Gabe and Meg tried to pull the quilt from the basket but it was stuck.

Suddenly Martha sat up and peeked out at them.

"Look!" cried Meg. "Martha was sleeping in our basket."

The first grade bunnies hopped
happily onto the stage. They tossed
their ears and raised their puppets high.
"That's my brother!" cried Mike.
He whistled at Matt and waved at
Martha.

Katie gently held up Martha's
basket.

"This is our bunny," she said.
"She lives in our classroom. She hops
around sometimes while we work. We
take care of her, and we love her."

"Floppy ears and hoppy feet,"
chanted the class. "We all think our
Martha's neat!"

"Hooray, Bunnies!" everyone
cheered.

Afterwards Mrs. Lee said proudly, "You are a great class with lots of spirit."

The children smiled at each other. They were happy to be first graders together.

# You Can Make A Bunny Puppet, Too!

You need a small paper bag with a flat bottom, white paper, scissors, tape, crayons or markers.

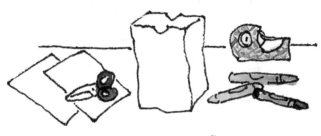

1. Fold the bag like this:

2. Draw your bunny's face on the bag's bottom.

3. Cut out two long, white paper ears.

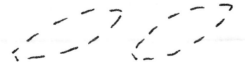

4. Tape the ears to the back of the bag.

5. If you wish, fold the
   ears down so they
   look like Martha's.

Put your hand inside the paper bag and bring your
bunny puppet to life.